T3-BPD-620

E
GA

Gage, Wilson

Down in the
boondocks

DATE			
MR 14 '79 Thompson 7-08			
T-9 10-06 Gonz			
10-06 Smith			
FE 4 '81 10-06 ℗			
FE MN 27 '82			
7-9			
T 13			
MY 14 '85			
73			
T6			
10-71 K			

Down in the boondocks
Gage, Wilson
E
NOT AR

© THE BAKER & TAYLOR CO.

WILSON GAGE

Down in the Boondocks

pictures by
GLEN ROUNDS

Greenwillow
Read-alone

GREENWILLOW BOOKS
A Division of William Morrow & Company, Inc., New York

2 3 4 5 6 7 8 9 10

Library of Congress Cataloging in Publication Data
Down in the boondocks. (Greenwillow read-alone)
Summary: Relates in rhyme what happens when
a thief decides to rob a deaf farmer.
[1. Deaf—Fiction. 2. Stories in rhyme]
I. Rounds, Glen (date) II. Title.
PZ8.3.S8127Do [E] 76-45380
ISBN 0-688-80085-8 ISBN 0-688-84085-X lib. bdg.

To Trudie Schafer

to read when she has finished

reading that other book

Down in the boondocks,

The boondocks, the boondocks,

There lives an old farmer

Who is deaf in one ear.

He is deaf in the other,

The other, the other.

He is deaf in the other

For most of the year.

He has an ear trumpet,

Ear trumpet, ear trumpet.

He has an ear trumpet

Which helps him to hear.

His wife has to holler,
To holler, to holler.
His wife has to holler,
"Come get your beer."

He has a fine rooster,

A rooster, a rooster.

He has a fine rooster

Who crows loud and clear.

But the farmer keeps snoring

And snoring and snoring.

If his wife didn't shake him

He would sleep for a year.

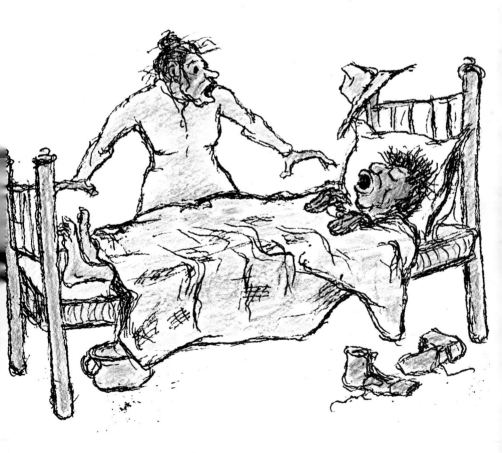

His wife has some hens,

Some white hens, some fat hens.

When one lays an egg

They all cackle with cheer.

But the farmer can't hear them,

He simply can't hear them.

"Those hens are not laying,"

He says with a sneer.

He has a good watchdog,

A bulldog, a watchdog.

It roars like a dragon

When strangers appear.

"You're not a good watchdog,"
Complains the old farmer.
"That bark's not enough
To fill a flea's ear."

He has an old wagon,

A broken-down wagon,

A worn-out old wagon

Which goes in low gear.

The wheels are all squealy

And squeaky and squawky.

They make such a racket

It sounds mighty queer.

But the farmer can't hear it,
Can't hear it, can't hear it.
And he drives his old wagon
From yonder to here.

He has a gray mule

With four legs and a swayback.

He has an old mule

With a tail in the rear.

The mule pulls the wagon,

The screechy old wagon.

It makes so much noise

The mule brays with fear.

Down in the boondocks,

The boondocks, the boondocks,

There lives an old farmer

Who is deaf in one ear.

He says, "It's so peaceful

Down here in the boondocks,

I'm glad I made farming

My whole life's career."

But early one morning

Down in the boondocks,

A robber came creeping

And crawling so near.

He came to steal chickens,

The white ones, the fat ones.

He came to steal eggs

And to drink all the beer.

The rooster was crowing

Because it was morning.

The rooster was crowing

So loud and so clear.

The hens were all laying,

The fat hens, the white hens.

They all laid their eggs

And they cackled with cheer.

The watchdog was barking,

The bulldog, the watchdog.

The watchdog was roaring

So strangers could hear.

The farmer was driving

His wagon, his wagon.

The four wheels were squealing

And sounding so queer.

ADRIAN PUBLIC SCHOOLS
Adrian, Michigan

The mule was soon bawling

And braying and bawling.

The mule started squalling

And bucked like a steer.

The wife had to holler
And holler and holler.
The wife had to holler
To make herself clear.
"Now here's your ear trumpet,
Ear trumpet, ear trumpet.
Now here's your ear trumpet
And here is your beer."

The robber stopped crawling

Along through the meadow.

He heard all the clatter

And trembled with fear.

He heard all the racket

And rumpus and rampage.

He turned from the boondocks

And ran like a deer.

"I'll never go back,"

Cried the robber, the robber.

"The boondocks are spooky

And scary and queer."

Down in the boondocks,

The boondocks, the boondocks,

The farmer said, "My, it is

Quiet down here.

The days are so calm

And the nights are so peaceful

If my wife didn't shake me

I could sleep for a year."

Now I'm glad I don't live
In the boondocks, the boondocks,
Close to that farmer
Who is deaf in one ear.